PRITHVIRAJ CHAUHAN

MUCH BEFORE THE ADVENT OF THE MUGHALS IN INDIA, DELHI WAS RULED BY A BRAVE KING, PRITHVIRAJ CHAUHAN.

DURING THE SAME PERIOD, KANNAUJ, A MUCH BIGGER AND MORE POWERFUL KINGDOM THAN DELHI, WAS RULED BY JAICHAND.

MAHARAJ, YOU HAVE ONLY TO PERFORM THE RAJASUYA YAGNA TO BECOME AN EMPEROR.

I WISH I WERE THE EMPEROR OF INDIA.

A GOOD IDEA. THOSE WHO DARE OPPOSE ME SHALL BE DESTROYED.

INFORM ALL THE KINGS THAT THEY SHOULD ACCEPT ME AS THEIR MASTER AND PARTICIPATE IN MY RAJASUYA YAGNA.

AS YOU WISH, MAHARAJ!

THE KINGS WHO REFUSED TO ACCEPT JAICHAND AS THEIR RULER HAD TO FACE THE MIGHT OF HIS FORCES.

FINALLY, JAICHAND WAS ACCEPTED AS THE SOLE RULER BY ALL THE KINGS EXCEPT ONE.

I AM GLAD THAT ALL THESE KINGS ACCEPT MY SUPREMACY... BUT WHAT ABOUT PRITHVIRAJ?

THE MESSENGER HAS NOT YET RETURNED, MAHARAJ.

PRITHVIRAJ BECAME VERY ANGRY WITH JAICHAND'S MESSENGER. HIS GURU SPOKE TO THE MESSENGER.

GO AND TELL YOUR MASTER THAT DELHI WILL HAVE ONLY PRITHVIRAJ AS ITS KING.

PRITHVIRAJ WAS SO UPSET BY WHAT HE HAD HEARD THAT TO DROWN HIS ANGER, HE WENT ON A HUNTING EXPEDITION.

MEANWHILE, JAICHAND'S MESSENGER HAD REACHED KANNAUJ.

MAHARAJ! PRITHVIRAJ HAS REFUSED TO ACCEPT YOUR SUPREMACY.

I SHALL ATTACK DELHI AND PUNISH HIM.

BUT MAHARAJ, THE DATE OF THE YAGNA IS VERY NEAR. WE DON'T HAVE ENOUGH TIME TO ATTACK DELHI.

YOU ARE RIGHT. I'LL WAIT TILL THE YAGNA IS OVER. ALONG WITH THE YAGNA I SHALL HOLD MY DAUGHTER SAMYOGITA'S SWAYAMVAR.

AT THE SWAYAMVAR, SAMYOGITA SHALL CHOOSE HER HUSBAND FROM AMONGST THE INVITED KINGS.

AND I HAVE AN EXCELLENT PLAN TO HUMILIATE PRITHVIRAJ AT THE SWAYAMVAR.

BUT HAVING LISTENED TO MANY TALES OF PRITHVIRAJ'S BRAVERY, SAMYOGITA HAD FALLEN IN LOVE WITH HIM WITHOUT EVEN MEETING HIM.

THE SWAYAMVAR SHALL NOT TAKE PLACE.

BUT YOUR FATHER HAS ALREADY INVITED MANY KINGS.

I WILL NOT CHOOSE ANY OF THEM. I HAVE ALREADY CHOSEN MAHARAJ PRITHVIRAJ.

BUT YOUR FATHER DOESN'T LIKE HIM.

WHY? BECAUSE HE HAD THE COURAGE TO OPPOSE MY FATHER. I'LL MARRY PRITHVIRAJ AND NONE OTHER.

THE NEWS OF BOTH, THE HUMILIATION PLANNED FOR HIM BY JAICHAND, AND SAMYOGITA'S LOVE FOR HIM REACHED PRITHVIRAJ.

CHAND, MY FRIEND, MY HONOUR IS AT STAKE. I MUST MARRY SAMYOGITA.

BUT HOW WILL YOU DO THAT, MAHARAJ?

JAICHAND WILL NOT LET ME ENTER KANNAUJ. BUT HE WILL NOT STOP A LEARNED MAN LIKE YOU.

SO CHAND PROCEEDED TO KANNAUJ WITH PRITHVIRAJ DISGUISED AS HIS BETEL-CARRIER AND A HUNDRED SELECTED WARRIORS ALSO DISGUISED AS SERVANTS.

AFTER SEVERAL DAYS, THEY REACHED KANNAUJ.

THAT SHINING GOLD-COVERED DOME IS JAICHAND'S PALACE, MAHARAJ!

DON'T CALL ME MAHARAJ. I AM SUPPOSED TO BE YOUR SERVANT.

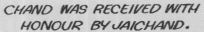

CHAND WAS RECEIVED WITH HONOUR BY JAICHAND.

I HAVE HEARD THAT PRITHVIRAJ IS A GOOD FIGHTER.

YES, HE CAN STRIKE FIFTY TIMES BEFORE HIS ENEMY EVEN RAISES HIS SWORD.

JAICHAND DID NOT LIKE CHAND'S REPLY BUT HE KEPT QUIET.

GO AND MAKE ARRANGEMENTS FOR OUR GUEST'S STAY.

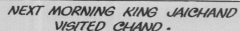

THEN JAICHAND RETIRED TO HIS PALACE.

NEXT MORNING KING JAICHAND VISITED CHAND.

I HOPE YOU ARE COMFORTABLE HERE.

WE ARE. PLEASE SIT DOWN.

JAICHAND WAS IMPRESSED BY THE PERSONALITY OF THE BETEL-CARRIER.

THIS MAN IS NOT AN ORDINARY SERVANT.

8

THERE IS SOMETHING STRANGE ABOUT THIS SERVANT.

WHILE GOING OUT, JAICHAND GLANCED THROUGH A WINDOW.

HE DOES NOT SEEM TO BE A SERVANT.

IMMEDIATELY JAICHAND ALERTED HIS FORCES.

GUARD ALL THE ROADS. KEEP AN EYE ON THOSE PEOPLE.

MEANWHILE, PRITHVIRAJ WAS PLANNING TO MEET SAMYOGITA.

WE CAN'T REMAIN SAFE HERE FOR LONG, SOMETHING MUST BE DONE SOON.

JAICHAND KNEW THAT HIS DAUGHTER HAD DECIDED TO MARRY PRITHVIRAJ AT ANY COST. HE QUICKLY CHANGED HIS PLANS.

MINISTER, INFORM ALL THE INVITED KINGS THAT THE SWAYAMWAR WILL TAKE PLACE TOMORROW, AND NOT WITH THE YAGNA, AS PLANNED EARLIER.

AS YOU WISH MAHARAJ.

AN EXCITED SOLDIER HURRIED TO PRITHVIRAJ.

MAHARAJ, WE HAVE NO TIME TO LOSE. THE SWAYAMWAR IS GOING TO TAKE PLACE TOMORROW.

SO SOON?

YES, AND JAICHAND IS GOING TO PLACE YOUR STATUE AT THE GATE TO HUMILIATE YOU.

HE SHALL PAY DEARLY FOR HUMILIATING ME THUS.

NEXT DAY AT THE SWAYAMWAR, PRITHVIRAJ'S STATUE WAS PLACED NEAR THE GATE AND SAMYOGITA WAS LED TO SELECT HER HUSBAND, FROM AMONG THE ASSEMBLED KINGS, ACCOMPANIED BY THEIR *CHARANS

I EXPECTED HIM TO BE PRESENT HERE IN DISGUISE...

WHAT SHALL I DO NOW...

FINALLY SAMYOGITA PUT THE GARLAND AROUND THE NECK OF PRITHVIRAJ'S STATUE.

MY HUSBAND CAN ONLY BE PRITHVIRAJ.

*CHARANS- POET WHO ACCOMPANIED KINGS TO SWAYAMWARS TO SING THEIR PRAISES WHEN THE PRINCES APPROACHED.

BUT WITHIN NO TIME JAICHAND'S HUGE ARMY HAD SURROUNDED THEM.

ATTACK AND CAPTURE PRITHVIRAJ AT ANY COST.

THE FIRST ATTACK ON PRITHVIRAJ WAS LED BY MIR BANDAN — A PERSIAN OFFICER IN JAICHAND'S ARMY.

BUT MIR BANDAN WAS NO MATCH FOR PRITHVIRAJ.

WITH MIR BANDAN'S DEATH, HIS SOLDIERS RAN HELTER-SKELTER.

THEN PRITHVIRAJ AND HIS SOLDIERS ATTACKED JAICHAND'S MAIN FORCES.

SOON PRITHVIRAJ WITH HIS
SOLDIERS CRASHED THROUGH
THE ENEMY LINES. THE SOLDIERS
WERE JUBILANT.

BUT THEIR JOY WAS SHORT LIVED.
CUNNING JAICHAND HAD PLACED
MORE SOLDIERS FARTHER DOWN
THE ROUTE.

THIS TIME PRITHVIRAJ WAS
SERIOUSLY INJURED. BUT HE PULLED
THE ARROW OUT.

THOUGH THEY PROVIDED SAFETY, THE HILLS CHECKED THE SPEED OF PRITHVIRAJ'S SOLDIERS. SO, THE ENEMY STARTED COMING CLOSER. ON A NARROW HILLY PATH —

WE WILL LEAVE ONE WARRIOR HERE TO ENGAGE THE ENEMY AND THE OTHERS WILL PROCEED TO DELHI.

NO..

... I AM NOT A COWARD, I WILL STAY HERE AND FACE THE ENEMY.

NOBODY CAN DOUBT YOUR BRAVERY, MAHARAJ. BUT OUR AIM IS NOT TO FIGHT THE ENEMY BUT TO AVENGE YOUR INSULT....

.... AND THAT PURPOSE WILL NOT BE ACHIEVED IF YOU DO NOT REACH DELHI WITH YOUR BRIDE.

AFTER QUITE SOME PERSUASION, PRITHVIRAJ AGREED AND THEY LEFT BAGH RAI BEHIND TO CHECK THE ENEMY.

BAGH RAI WAS A FIERCE FIGHTER.

BUT HE WAS GREATLY OUTNUMBERED.

AFTER THE DEATH OF BAGH RAI, THE JUBILANT FORCES OF THE ENEMY RUSHED FORWARD.

BEWARE! THERE IS ANOTHER BLOCKING THE PATH.

MANY WERE THE LIVES, SACRIFICED FOR PRITHVIRAJ.

KANH, THE COMMANDER OF PRITHVIRAJ'S ARMY, DECIDED TO CHECK THE ENEMY HIMSELF.

EVEN KANH'S HORSE ATTACKED THE ENEMY.

AFTER A BITTER FIGHT—

THERE! HE TOO IS KILLED.

NOW WE CAN CAPTURE PRITHVIRAJ WITH EASE.

BUT BY THEN, IT WAS TOO LATE. PRITHVIRAJ HAD REACHED HIS FORT IN DELHI.

AFRAID TO FIGHT PRITHVIRAJ'S VAST ARMY, THE FRUSTRATED JAICHAND WENT BACK.

THERE WAS GREAT REJOICING IN DELHI.

LONG LIVE MAHARAJ PRITHVIRAJ. LONG LIVE MAHARANI SAMYOGITA.

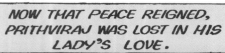

NOW THAT PEACE REIGNED, PRITHVIRAJ WAS LOST IN HIS LADY'S LOVE.

WE HAVE NOT SEEN OUR KING FOR A LONG TIME.

HE DOESN'T EVEN COME OUT OF HIS PALACE.

EVERYONE IS UNHAPPY.

YES, OUR KING HAS NOT COME TO THE COURT SINCE HE GOT MARRIED.

PRITHVIRAJ'S GURU WAS ALSO UNHAPPY.

IT IS A PITY THAT A BRAVE, FEARLESS NOBLE WARRIOR LIKE PRITHVIRAJ SHOULD CARE SO MUCH FOR A WOMAN AND FORGET HIS DUTIES.

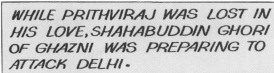

BUT SAMYOGITA IS NOT AN ORDINARY WOMAN.

NOR ARE THE PROBLEMS OF THE STATE ORDINARY.

WHILE PRITHVIRAJ WAS LOST IN HIS LOVE, SHAHABUDDIN GHORI OF GHAZNI WAS PREPARING TO ATTACK DELHI.

ALL THE SEVEN TIMES PRITHVIRAJ HAD DEFEATED, CAPTURED AND VERY GEN- EROUSLY RELEASED GHORI TO SEND HIM BACK HOME.

THIS TIME GHORI WAS CONFIDENT OF VICTORY AS JAICHAND HAD PROMISED TO HELP HIM IF NECESSARY.

JAICHAND IS MY ALLY. THIS IS MY CHANCE TO DEFEAT PRITHVIRAJ.

AND THUS WITH THE HELP OF THE TREACHEROUS JAICHAND SHAHABUDDIN THIS TIME RAISED A MUCH LARGER FORCE.

THE NOBLES OF DELHI WERE WORRIED BY THE ADVANCE OF SHAHABUDDIN'S FORCES.

BUT HOW CAN WE INFORM THE KING? HE GETS ANGRY WHEN DISTURBED.

I WILL WRITE HIM A LETTER.

A LETTER FROM MY GURU... WHY?

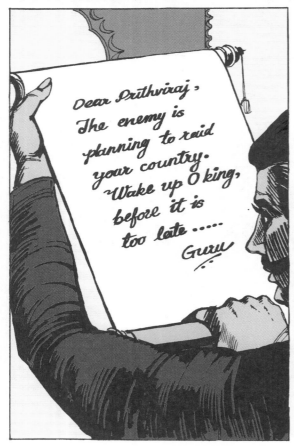

Dear Prithviraj,
The enemy is planning to raid your country. Wake up O king, before it is too late .....
Guru

SHAME ON ME! I NEGLECTED MY DUTIES AS A KING.

PRITHVIRAJ'S FORCES HAD GROWN WEAK AS HE HAD LOST THE COMMANDER AND THE CREAM OF HIS WARRIORS IN THE BATTLE WITH JAICHAND. BUT HE GATHERED THE REMAINING SOLDIERS AND LED THEM TO FACE THE ENEMY.

SHAHABUDDIN GHORI'S FORCES WERE LED BY THREE VETERAN OFFICERS.

SOON THE TWO ARMIES WERE FIGHTING EACH OTHER.

PRITHVIRAJ AND HIS SOLDIERS FOUGHT WITH EXCEPTIONAL BRAVERY.

BUT PRITHVIRAJ'S SMALL FORCE WAS MASSACRED AND HE WAS CAPTURED BY GHORI'S SOLDIERS.

CAPTIVE PRITHVIRAJ WAS TAKEN TO GHAZNI.

LOOK AT THE FIERCE LION OF DELHI.

HA! HA

LOWER YOUR EYES, YOU INFIDEL. HOW DARE YOU STARE AT ME?

UNAFRAID, PRITHVIRAJ CONTINUED TO STARE.

GUARDS! DESTROY HIS EYES!

AND SO PRITHVIRAJ'S EYES WERE BURNT.

WHEN POET CHAND HEARD ABOUT PRITHVIRAJ'S FATE, HE DRESSED AS A SADHU AND STARTED AT ONCE FOR GHAZNI.

CHAND MET SHAHABUDDIN WHEN HE WAS PRACTISING ARCHERY.

WHAT DO YOU THINK OF MY AIM?

GOOD, BUT VERY ORDINARY COMPARED TO MAHARAJ PRITHVIRAJ'S SKILL...

.... HE CAN PIERCE A METAL GONG WITH A HEADLESS ARROW.

IMPOSSIBLE.

IT IS NOT IMPOSSIBLE. ALTHOUGH HE IS BLIND HE CAN DO IT, GUIDED ONLY BY THE SOUND OF THE GONG.

I WANT TO SEE IT, BUT IF HE FAILS, YOUR HEAD WILL BE CUT OFF.

CHAND MET PRITHVIRAJ IN THE PRISON AND TOLD HIM OF HIS PLAN.

YOU CAN KILL SHAHABUDDIN DURING THE DEMONSTRATION AND AVENGE YOUR INSULT. AND THEN WE CAN STAB EACH OTHER.

BUT HOW WILL I KNOW WHERE HE IS SITTING.

LEAVE THAT TO ME.

ALL RIGHT

MAHARAJ PRITHVIRAJ HAS TO GIVE A DEMONSTRATION. BUT SINCE HE IS A KING, HE WILL NOT OBEY A COMMON MAN'S ORDER. YOU WILL HAVE TO ORDER HIM TO SHOOT.

AGREED

AT THE COURT, NEXT DAY—

READY....AIM

AT THE LAST ORDER, PRITHVIRAJ WHIRLED ROUND AND AIMED AT SHAHABUDDIN GUIDED BY HIS VOICE.

SHOOT.....aaa...ah

PRITHVIRAJ LEARNT FROM HIS KEEN SENSE OF HEARING THAT HIS ENEMY WAS DEAD.

TO AVOID A HUMILIATING DEATH AT THE HANDS OF ENEMY SOLDIERS CHAND AND PRITHVIRAJ STABBED EACH OTHER AS PREVIOUSLY PLANNED.

VICTORY TO MAHARAJ PRITHVIRAJ.